BARRACK-ROOM BALLADS

By RUDYARD KIPLING

1913

Dedication

To T. A.
I have made for you a song,
And it may be right or wrong,
But only you can tell me if it's true;
I have tried for to explain
Both your pleasure and your pain,
And, Thomas, here's my best respects to you!

O there'll surely come a day
When they'll give you all your pay,
And treat you as a Christian ought to do;
So, until that day comes round,
Heaven keep you safe and sound,
And, Thomas, here's my best respects to you!
R. K.

This book has been published by:

Contact: sales@nuvisionpublications.com

URL: http://www.nuvisionpublications.com

Publishing Date: 2008

ISBN# 1-59547-621-0

Please see our website for several books created for
education, research and entertainment.

Specializing in rare, out-of-print books still in demand.

NuVision Publications, LLC is dedicated to bringing new life to rare, historic, and formerly out-of-print books. Most re-print publishers simply photocopy, or scan and print the pages from the original book, which can make the book hard to read as most re-print books are 100+ years old. It is our policy to take the time to convert the original faded, sometimes blotched text into crisp, clear digital text. All of our printed books have been completely reformatted to be easy to read and enjoy.

Please note that we do not correct out-of-date facts or grammar-type errors that were in the original book. We do our best to retain the original composition of the text, the way the author intended it.

NuVision Publications, LLC
Sioux Falls, SD USA

CONTENTS

FIRST SERIES (1892)

Danny Deever

"What are the bugles blowin' for?" said Files-on-Parade.
"To turn you out, to turn you out", the Colour-Sergeant said.
"What makes you look so white, so white?" said Files-on-Parade.
"I'm dreadin' what I've got to watch", the Colour-Sergeant said.
   For they're hangin' Danny Deever, you can hear the Dead March play,
   The regiment's in 'ollow square -- they're hangin' him to-day;
   They've taken of his buttons off an' cut his stripes away,
   An' they're hangin' Danny Deever in the mornin'.

"What makes the rear-rank breathe so 'ard?" said Files-on-Parade.
"It's bitter cold, it's bitter cold", the Colour-Sergeant said.
"What makes that front-rank man fall down?" said Files-on-Parade.
"A touch o' sun, a touch o' sun", the Colour-Sergeant said.
   They are hangin' Danny Deever, they are marchin' of 'im round,
   They 'ave 'alted Danny Deever by 'is coffin on the ground;
   An' 'e'll swing in 'arf a minute for a sneakin' shootin' hound --
   O they're hangin' Danny Deever in the mornin'!

"'Is cot was right-'and cot to mine", said Files-on-Parade.
"'E's sleepin' out an' far to-night", the Colour-Sergeant said.
"I've drunk 'is beer a score o' times", said Files-on-Parade.
"'E's drinkin' bitter beer alone", the Colour-Sergeant said.
   They are hangin' Danny Deever, you must mark 'im to 'is place,
   For 'e shot a comrade sleepin' -- you must look 'im in the face;
   Nine 'undred of 'is county an' the regiment's disgrace,
   While they're hangin' Danny Deever in the mornin'.

"What's that so black agin' the sun?" said Files-on-Parade.
"It's Danny fightin' 'ard for life", the Colour-Sergeant said.
"What's that that whimpers over'ead?" said Files-on-Parade.
"It's Danny's soul that's passin' now", the Colour-Sergeant said.
   For they're done with Danny Deever, you can 'ear the quickstep play,
   The regiment's in column, an' they're marchin' us away;
   Ho! the young recruits are shakin', an' they'll want their beer to-day,
   After hangin' Danny Deever in the mornin'.

Tommy

I went into a public-'ouse to get a pint o' beer,
The publican 'e up an' sez, "We serve no red-coats here."
The girls be'ind the bar they laughed an' giggled fit to die,
I outs into the street again an' to myself sez I:
 O it's Tommy this, an' Tommy that, an' "Tommy, go away";
 But it's "Thank you, Mister Atkins", when the band begins to play,
 The band begins to play, my boys, the band begins to play,
 O it's "Thank you, Mister Atkins", when the band begins to play.

I went into a theatre as sober as could be,
They gave a drunk civilian room, but 'adn't none for me;
They sent me to the gallery or round the music-'alls,
But when it comes to fightin', Lord! they'll shove me in the stalls!
 For it's Tommy this, an' Tommy that, an' "Tommy, wait outside";
 But it's "Special train for Atkins" when the trooper's on the tide,
 The troopship's on the tide, my boys, the troopship's on the tide,
 O it's "Special train for Atkins" when the trooper's on the tide.

Yes, makin' mock o' uniforms that guard you while you sleep
Is cheaper than them uniforms, an' they're starvation cheap;
An' hustlin' drunken soldiers when they're goin' large a bit
Is five times better business than paradin' in full kit.
 Then it's Tommy this, an' Tommy that, an' "Tommy, 'ow's yer soul?"
 But it's "Thin red line of 'eroes" when the drums begin to roll,
 The drums begin to roll, my boys, the drums begin to roll,
 O it's "Thin red line of 'eroes" when the drums begin to roll.

We aren't no thin red 'eroes, nor we aren't no blackguards too,
But single men in barricks, most remarkable like you;
An' if sometimes our conduck isn't all your fancy paints,
Why, single men in barricks don't grow into plaster saints;
 While it's Tommy this, an' Tommy that, an' "Tommy, fall be'ind",
 But it's "Please to walk in front, sir", when there's trouble in the wind,
 There's trouble in the wind, my boys, there's trouble in the wind,
 O it's "Please to walk in front, sir", when there's trouble in the wind.

You talk o' better food for us, an' schools, an' fires, an' all:
We'll wait for extry rations if you treat us rational.
Don't mess about the cook-room slops, but prove it to our face
The Widow's Uniform is not the soldier-man's disgrace.
 For it's Tommy this, an' Tommy that, an' "Chuck him out, the brute!"
 But it's "Saviour of 'is country" when the guns begin to shoot;
 An' it's Tommy this, an' Tommy that, an' anything you please;
 An' Tommy ain't a bloomin' fool -- you bet that Tommy sees!

Fuzzy-Wuzzy

(Soudan Expeditionary Force)

We've fought with many men acrost the seas,
  An' some of 'em was brave an' some was not:
The Paythan an' the Zulu an' Burmese;
  But the Fuzzy was the finest o' the lot.
We never got a ha'porth's change of 'im:
  'E squatted in the scrub an' 'ocked our 'orses,
'E cut our sentries up at Suakim,
  An' 'e played the cat an' banjo with our forces.
    So 'ere's to you, Fuzzy-Wuzzy, at your 'ome in the Soudan;
    You're a pore benighted 'eathen but a first-class fightin' man;
    We gives you your certificate, an' if you want it signed
    We'll come an' 'ave a romp with you whenever you're inclined.

We took our chanst among the Khyber 'ills,
  The Boers knocked us silly at a mile,
The Burman give us Irriwaddy chills,
  An' a Zulu impi dished us up in style:
But all we ever got from such as they
  Was pop to what the Fuzzy made us swaller;
We 'eld our bloomin' own, the papers say,
  But man for man the Fuzzy knocked us 'oller.
    Then 'ere's to you, Fuzzy-Wuzzy, an' the missis and the kid;
    Our orders was to break you, an' of course we went an' did.
    We sloshed you with Martinis, an' it wasn't 'ardly fair;
    But for all the odds agin' you, Fuzzy-Wuz, you broke the square.

'E 'asn't got no papers of 'is own,
  'E 'asn't got no medals nor rewards,
So we must certify the skill 'e's shown
  In usin' of 'is long two-'anded swords:
When 'e's 'oppin' in an' out among the bush
  With 'is coffin-'eaded shield an' shovel-spear,
An 'appy day with Fuzzy on the rush
  Will last an 'ealthy Tommy for a year.
    So 'ere's to you, Fuzzy-Wuzzy, an' your friends which are no more,
    If we 'adn't lost some messmates we would 'elp you to deplore;
    But give an' take's the gospel, an' we'll call the bargain fair,
    For if you 'ave lost more than us, you crumpled up the square!

'E rushes at the smoke when we let drive,
  An', before we know, 'e's 'ackin' at our 'ead;
'E's all 'ot sand an' ginger when alive,
  An' 'e's generally shammin' when 'e's dead.
'E's a daisy, 'e's a ducky, 'e's a lamb!
  'E's a injia-rubber idiot on the spree,
'E's the on'y thing that doesn't give a damn

For a Regiment o' British Infantree!
　So 'ere's to you, Fuzzy-Wuzzy, at your 'ome in the Soudan;
　You're a pore benighted 'eathen but a first-class fightin' man;
　An' 'ere's to you, Fuzzy-Wuzzy, with your 'ayrick 'ead of 'air --
　You big black boundin' beggar -- for you broke a British square!

Soldier, Soldier

"Soldier, soldier come from the wars,
Why don't you march with my true love?"
"We're fresh from off the ship an' 'e's maybe give the slip,
An' you'd best go look for a new love."
 New love! True love!
 Best go look for a new love,
 The dead they cannot rise, an' you'd better dry your eyes,
 An' you'd best go look for a new love.

"Soldier, soldier come from the wars,
What did you see o' my true love?"
"I seed 'im serve the Queen in a suit o' rifle-green,
An' you'd best go look for a new love."

"Soldier, soldier come from the wars,
Did ye see no more o' my true love?"
"I seed 'im runnin' by when the shots begun to fly --
But you'd best go look for a new love."

"Soldier, soldier come from the wars,
Did aught take 'arm to my true love?"
"I couldn't see the fight, for the smoke it lay so white --
An' you'd best go look for a new love."

"Soldier, soldier come from the wars,
I'll up an' tend to my true love!"
"'E's lying on the dead with a bullet through 'is 'ead,
An' you'd best go look for a new love."

"Soldier, soldier come from the wars,
I'll down an' die with my true love!"
"The pit we dug'll 'ide 'im an' the twenty men beside 'im --
An' you'd best go look for a new love."

"Soldier, soldier come from the wars,
Do you bring no sign from my true love?"
"I bring a lock of 'air that 'e allus used to wear,
An' you'd best go look for a new love."

"Soldier, soldier come from the wars,
O then I know it's true I've lost my true love!"
"An' I tell you truth again -- when you've lost the feel o' pain
You'd best take me for your true love."
 True love! New love!
 Best take 'im for a new love,
 The dead they cannot rise, an' you'd better dry your eyes,
 An' you'd best take 'im for your true love.

Screw-Guns

Smokin' my pipe on the mountings, sniffin' the mornin' cool,
I walks in my old brown gaiters along o' my old brown mule,
With seventy gunners be'ind me, an' never a beggar forgets
It's only the pick of the Army
      that handles the dear little pets -- 'Tss! 'Tss!
  For you all love the screw-guns -- the screw-guns they all love you!
  So when we call round with a few guns,
      o' course you will know what to do -- hoo! hoo!
  Jest send in your Chief an' surrender --
      it's worse if you fights or you runs:
  You can go where you please, you can skid up the trees,
      but you don't get away from the guns!

They sends us along where the roads are, but mostly we goes where they ain't:
We'd climb up the side of a sign-board an' trust to the stick o' the paint:
We've chivied the Naga an' Looshai, we've give the Afreedeeman fits,
For we fancies ourselves at two thousand,
      we guns that are built in two bits -- 'Tss! 'Tss!
  For you all love the screw-guns . . .

If a man doesn't work, why, we drills 'im an' teaches 'im 'ow to behave;
If a beggar can't march, why, we kills 'im an' rattles 'im into 'is grave.
You've got to stand up to our business an' spring without snatchin' or fuss.
D'you say that you sweat with the field-guns?
      By God, you must lather with us -- 'Tss! 'Tss!
  For you all love the screw-guns . . .

The eagles is screamin' around us, the river's a-moanin' below,
We're clear o' the pine an' the oak-scrub,
      we're out on the rocks an' the snow,
An' the wind is as thin as a whip-lash what carries away to the plains
The rattle an' stamp o' the lead-mules --
      the jinglety-jink o' the chains -- 'Tss! 'Tss!
  For you all love the screw-guns . . .

There's a wheel on the Horns o' the Mornin',
      an' a wheel on the edge o' the Pit,
An' a drop into nothin' beneath you as straight as a beggar can spit:
With the sweat runnin' out o' your shirt-sleeves,
      an' the sun off the snow in your face,
An' 'arf o' the men on the drag-ropes
      to hold the old gun in 'er place -- 'Tss! 'Tss!
  For you all love the screw-guns . . .

Smokin' my pipe on the mountings, sniffin' the mornin' cool,
I climbs in my old brown gaiters along o' my old brown mule.
The monkey can say what our road was --
      the wild-goat 'e knows where we passed.

Stand easy, you long-eared old darlin's!
    Out drag-ropes! With shrapnel! Hold fast -- 'Tss! 'Tss!
For you all love the screw-guns -- the screw-guns they all love you!
So when we take tea with a few guns,
    o' course you will know what to do -- hoo! hoo!
Jest send in your Chief an' surrender --
    it's worse if you fights or you runs:
You may hide in the caves, they'll be only your graves,
    but you can't get away from the guns!

Cells

I've a head like a concertina: I've a tongue like a button-stick:
I've a mouth like an old potato, and I'm more than a little sick,
But I've had my fun o' the Corp'ral's Guard: I've made the cinders fly,
And I'm here in the Clink for a thundering drink
     and blacking the Corporal's eye.
  With a second-hand overcoat under my head,
  And a beautiful view of the yard,
 O it's pack-drill for me and a fortnight's C.B.
  For "drunk and resisting the Guard!"
  Mad drunk and resisting the Guard --
  'Strewth, but I socked it them hard!
 So it's pack-drill for me and a fortnight's C.B.
  For "drunk and resisting the Guard."

I started o' canteen porter, I finished o' canteen beer,
But a dose o' gin that a mate slipped in, it was that that brought me here.
'Twas that and an extry double Guard that rubbed my nose in the dirt;
But I fell away with the Corp'ral's stock
     and the best of the Corp'ral's shirt.

I left my cap in a public-house, my boots in the public road,
And Lord knows where, and I don't care, my belt and my tunic goed;
They'll stop my pay, they'll cut away the stripes I used to wear,
But I left my mark on the Corp'ral's face, and I think he'll keep it there!

My wife she cries on the barrack-gate, my kid in the barrack-yard,
It ain't that I mind the Ord'ly room -- it's that that cuts so hard.
I'll take my oath before them both that I will sure abstain,
But as soon as I'm in with a mate and gin, I know I'll do it again!
  With a second-hand overcoat under my head,
  And a beautiful view of the yard,
 Yes, it's pack-drill for me and a fortnight's C.B.
  For "drunk and resisting the Guard!"
  Mad drunk and resisting the Guard --
  'Strewth, but I socked it them hard!
 So it's pack-drill for me and a fortnight's C.B.
  For "drunk and resisting the Guard."

Gunga Din

You may talk o' gin and beer
When you're quartered safe out 'ere,
An' you're sent to penny-fights an' Aldershot it;
But when it comes to slaughter
You will do your work on water,
An' you'll lick the bloomin' boots of 'im that's got it.
Now in Injia's sunny clime,
Where I used to spend my time
A-servin' of 'Er Majesty the Queen,
Of all them blackfaced crew
The finest man I knew
Was our regimental bhisti, Gunga Din.
    He was "Din! Din! Din!
  You limpin' lump o' brick-dust, Gunga Din!
    Hi! slippery hitherao!
    Water, get it! Panee lao!
  You squidgy-nosed old idol, Gunga Din."

The uniform 'e wore
Was nothin' much before,
An' rather less than 'arf o' that be'ind,
For a piece o' twisty rag
An' a goatskin water-bag
Was all the field-equipment 'e could find.
When the sweatin' troop-train lay
In a sidin' through the day,
Where the 'eat would make your bloomin' eyebrows crawl,
We shouted "Harry By!"
Till our throats were bricky-dry,
Then we wopped 'im 'cause 'e couldn't serve us all.
    It was "Din! Din! Din!
  You 'eathen, where the mischief 'ave you been?
    You put some juldee in it
    Or I'll marrow you this minute
  If you don't fill up my helmet, Gunga Din!"

'E would dot an' carry one
Till the longest day was done;
An' 'e didn't seem to know the use o' fear.
If we charged or broke or cut,
You could bet your bloomin' nut,
'E'd be waitin' fifty paces right flank rear.
With 'is mussick on 'is back,
'E would skip with our attack,
An' watch us till the bugles made "Retire",
An' for all 'is dirty 'ide
'E was white, clear white, inside
When 'e went to tend the wounded under fire!
    It was "Din! Din! Din!"

With the bullets kickin' dust-spots on the green.
    When the cartridges ran out,
    You could hear the front-files shout,
  "Hi! ammunition-mules an' Gunga Din!"

I shan't forgit the night
When I dropped be'ind the fight
With a bullet where my belt-plate should 'a' been.
I was chokin' mad with thirst,
An' the man that spied me first
Was our good old grinnin', gruntin' Gunga Din.
'E lifted up my 'ead,
An' he plugged me where I bled,
An' 'e guv me 'arf-a-pint o' water-green:
It was crawlin' and it stunk,
But of all the drinks I've drunk,
I'm gratefullest to one from Gunga Din.
    It was "Din! Din! Din!
  'Ere's a beggar with a bullet through 'is spleen;
    'E's chawin' up the ground,
    An' 'e's kickin' all around:
  For Gawd's sake git the water, Gunga Din!"

'E carried me away
To where a dooli lay,
An' a bullet come an' drilled the beggar clean.
'E put me safe inside,
An' just before 'e died,
"I 'ope you liked your drink", sez Gunga Din.
So I'll meet 'im later on
At the place where 'e is gone --
Where it's always double drill and no canteen;
'E'll be squattin' on the coals
Givin' drink to poor damned souls,
An' I'll get a swig in hell from Gunga Din!
    Yes, Din! Din! Din!
  You Lazarushian-leather Gunga Din!
    Though I've belted you and flayed you,
    By the livin' Gawd that made you,
  You're a better man than I am, Gunga Din!

Oonts

(Northern India Transport Train)

Wot makes the soldier's 'eart to penk, wot makes 'im to perspire?
It isn't standin' up to charge nor lyin' down to fire;
But it's everlastin' waitin' on a everlastin' road
For the commissariat camel an' 'is commissariat load.
   O the oont, O the oont, O the commissariat oont!
    With 'is silly neck a-bobbin' like a basket full o' snakes;
   We packs 'im like an idol, an' you ought to 'ear 'im grunt,
    An' when we gets 'im loaded up 'is blessed girth-rope breaks.

Wot makes the rear-guard swear so 'ard when night is drorin' in,
An' every native follower is shiverin' for 'is skin?
It ain't the chanst o' being rushed by Paythans from the 'ills,
It's the commissariat camel puttin' on 'is bloomin' frills!
   O the oont, O the oont, O the hairy scary oont!
    A-trippin' over tent-ropes when we've got the night alarm!
   We socks 'im with a stretcher-pole an' 'eads 'im off in front,
    An' when we've saved 'is bloomin' life 'e chaws our bloomin' arm.

The 'orse 'e knows above a bit, the bullock's but a fool,
The elephant's a gentleman, the battery-mule's a mule;
But the commissariat cam-u-el, when all is said an' done,
'E's a devil an' a ostrich an' a orphan-child in one.
   O the oont, O the oont, O the Gawd-forsaken oont!
    The lumpy-'umpy 'ummin'-bird a-singin' where 'e lies,
   'E's blocked the whole division from the rear-guard to the front,
    An' when we get him up again -- the beggar goes an' dies!

'E'll gall an' chafe an' lame an' fight -- 'e smells most awful vile;
'E'll lose 'isself for ever if you let 'im stray a mile;
'E's game to graze the 'ole day long an' 'owl the 'ole night through,
An' when 'e comes to greasy ground 'e splits 'isself in two.
   O the oont, O the oont, O the floppin', droppin' oont!
    When 'is long legs give from under an' 'is meltin' eye is dim,
   The tribes is up be'ind us, and the tribes is out in front --
    It ain't no jam for Tommy, but it's kites an' crows for 'im.

So when the cruel march is done, an' when the roads is blind,
An' when we sees the camp in front an' 'ears the shots be'ind,
Ho! then we strips 'is saddle off, and all 'is woes is past:
'E thinks on us that used 'im so, and gets revenge at last.
   O the oont, O the oont, O the floatin', bloatin' oont!
    The late lamented camel in the water-cut 'e lies;
   We keeps a mile be'ind 'im an' we keeps a mile in front,
    But 'e gets into the drinkin'-casks, and then o' course we dies.

Loot

If you've ever stole a pheasant-egg be'ind the keeper's back,
 If you've ever snigged the washin' from the line,
If you've ever crammed a gander in your bloomin' 'aversack,
 You will understand this little song o' mine.
But the service rules are 'ard, an' from such we are debarred,
 For the same with English morals does not suit.
  (Cornet: Toot! toot!)
W'y, they call a man a robber if 'e stuffs 'is marchin' clobber
With the --
(Chorus) Loo! loo! Lulu! lulu! Loo! loo! Loot! loot! loot!
     Ow the loot!
     Bloomin' loot!
   That's the thing to make the boys git up an' shoot!
   It's the same with dogs an' men,
   If you'd make 'em come again
   Clap 'em forward with a Loo! loo! Lulu! Loot!
  (ff) Whoopee! Tear 'im, puppy! Loo! loo! Lulu! Loot! loot! loot!

If you've knocked a nigger edgeways when 'e's thrustin' for your life,
 You must leave 'im very careful where 'e fell;
An' may thank your stars an' gaiters if you didn't feel 'is knife
 That you ain't told off to bury 'im as well.
Then the sweatin' Tommies wonder as they spade the beggars under
 Why lootin' should be entered as a crime;
So if my song you'll 'ear, I will learn you plain an' clear
 'Ow to pay yourself for fightin' overtime.
(Chorus) With the loot, . . .

Now remember when you're 'acking round a gilded Burma god
 That 'is eyes is very often precious stones;
An' if you treat a nigger to a dose o' cleanin'-rod
 'E's like to show you everything 'e owns.
When 'e won't prodooce no more, pour some water on the floor
 Where you 'ear it answer 'ollow to the boot
  (Cornet: Toot! toot!) --
When the ground begins to sink, shove your baynick down the chink,
 An' you're sure to touch the --
(Chorus) Loo! loo! Lulu! Loot! loot! loot!
     Ow the loot! . . .

When from 'ouse to 'ouse you're 'unting, you must always work in pairs --
 It 'alves the gain, but safer you will find --
For a single man gets bottled on them twisty-wisty stairs,
 An' a woman comes and clobs 'im from be'ind.
When you've turned 'em inside out, an' it seems beyond a doubt
 As if there weren't enough to dust a flute
  (Cornet: Toot! toot!) --
Before you sling your 'ook, at the 'ousetops take a look,
 For it's underneath the tiles they 'ide the loot.

(Chorus) Ow the loot! . . .

You can mostly square a Sergint an' a Quartermaster too,
 If you only take the proper way to go;
I could never keep my pickin's, but I've learned you all I knew --
 An' don't you never say I told you so.
An' now I'll bid good-bye, for I'm gettin' rather dry,
 An' I see another tunin' up to toot
    (Cornet: Toot! toot!) --
So 'ere's good-luck to those that wears the Widow's clo'es,
 An' the Devil send 'em all they want o' loot!
(Chorus)   Yes, the loot,
                Bloomin' loot!
          In the tunic an' the mess-tin an' the boot!
          It's the same with dogs an' men,
          If you'd make 'em come again
    (fff) Whoop 'em forward with a Loo! loo! Lulu! Loot! loot! loot!
          Heeya! Sick 'im, puppy! Loo! loo! Lulu! Loot! loot! loot!

'Snarleyow'

This 'appened in a battle to a batt'ry of the corps
Which is first among the women an' amazin' first in war;
An' what the bloomin' battle was I don't remember now,
But Two's off-lead 'e answered to the name o' Snarleyow.
   Down in the Infantry, nobody cares;
   Down in the Cavalry, Colonel 'e swears;
   But down in the lead with the wheel at the flog
   Turns the bold Bombardier to a little whipped dog!

They was movin' into action, they was needed very sore,
To learn a little schoolin' to a native army corps,
They 'ad nipped against an uphill, they was tuckin' down the brow,
When a tricky, trundlin' roundshot give the knock to Snarleyow.

They cut 'im loose an' left 'im -- 'e was almost tore in two --
But he tried to follow after as a well-trained 'orse should do;
'E went an' fouled the limber, an' the Driver's Brother squeals:
"Pull up, pull up for Snarleyow -- 'is head's between 'is 'eels!"

The Driver 'umped 'is shoulder, for the wheels was goin' round,
An' there ain't no "Stop, conductor!" when a batt'ry's changin' ground;
Sez 'e: "I broke the beggar in, an' very sad I feels,
But I couldn't pull up, not for you -- your 'ead between your 'eels!"

'E 'adn't 'ardly spoke the word, before a droppin' shell
A little right the batt'ry an' between the sections fell;
An' when the smoke 'ad cleared away, before the limber wheels,
There lay the Driver's Brother with 'is 'ead between 'is 'eels.

Then sez the Driver's Brother, an' 'is words was very plain,
"For Gawd's own sake get over me, an' put me out o' pain."
They saw 'is wounds was mortial, an' they judged that it was best,
So they took an' drove the limber straight across 'is back an' chest.

The Driver 'e give nothin' 'cept a little coughin' grunt,
But 'e swung 'is 'orses 'andsome when it came to "Action Front!"
An' if one wheel was juicy, you may lay your Monday head
'Twas juicier for the niggers when the case begun to spread.

The moril of this story, it is plainly to be seen:
You 'avn't got no families when servin' of the Queen --
You 'avn't got no brothers, fathers, sisters, wives, or sons --
If you want to win your battles take an' work your bloomin' guns!
   Down in the Infantry, nobody cares;
   Down in the Cavalry, Colonel 'e swears;
   But down in the lead with the wheel at the flog
   Turns the bold Bombardier to a little whipped dog!

The Widow at Windsor

'Ave you 'eard o' the Widow at Windsor
 With a hairy gold crown on 'er 'ead?
She 'as ships on the foam -- she 'as millions at 'ome,
 An' she pays us poor beggars in red.
   (Ow, poor beggars in red!)
There's 'er nick on the cavalry 'orses,
 There's 'er mark on the medical stores --
An' 'er troopers you'll find with a fair wind be'ind
 That takes us to various wars.
   (Poor beggars! -- barbarious wars!)
     Then 'ere's to the Widow at Windsor,
      An' 'ere's to the stores an' the guns,
     The men an' the 'orses what makes up the forces
      O' Missis Victorier's sons.
     (Poor beggars! Victorier's sons!)

Walk wide o' the Widow at Windsor,
 For 'alf o' Creation she owns:
We 'ave bought 'er the same with the sword an' the flame,
 An' we've salted it down with our bones.
   (Poor beggars! -- it's blue with our bones!)
Hands off o' the sons o' the Widow,
 Hands off o' the goods in 'er shop,
For the Kings must come down an' the Emperors frown
 When the Widow at Windsor says "Stop"!
   (Poor beggars! -- we're sent to say "Stop"!)
     Then 'ere's to the Lodge o' the Widow,
      From the Pole to the Tropics it runs --
     To the Lodge that we tile with the rank an' the file,
      An' open in form with the guns.
     (Poor beggars! -- it's always they guns!)

We 'ave 'eard o' the Widow at Windsor,
 It's safest to let 'er alone:
For 'er sentries we stand by the sea an' the land
 Wherever the bugles are blown.
   (Poor beggars! -- an' don't we get blown!)
Take 'old o' the Wings o' the Mornin',
 An' flop round the earth till you're dead;
But you won't get away from the tune that they play
 To the bloomin' old rag over'ead.
   (Poor beggars! -- it's 'ot over'ead!)
     Then 'ere's to the sons o' the Widow,
      Wherever, 'owever they roam.
     'Ere's all they desire, an' if they require
      A speedy return to their 'ome.
     (Poor beggars! -- they'll never see 'ome!)

Belts

There was a row in Silver Street that's near to Dublin Quay,
Between an Irish regiment an' English cavalree;
It started at Revelly an' it lasted on till dark:
The first man dropped at Harrison's, the last forninst the Park.
    For it was: -- "Belts, belts, belts, an' that's one for you!"
    An' it was "Belts, belts, belts, an' that's done for you!"
    O buckle an' tongue
    Was the song that we sung
    From Harrison's down to the Park!

There was a row in Silver Street -- the regiments was out,
They called us "Delhi Rebels", an' we answered "Threes about!"
That drew them like a hornet's nest -- we met them good an' large,
The English at the double an' the Irish at the charge.
    Then it was: -- "Belts . . .

There was a row in Silver Street -- an' I was in it too;
We passed the time o' day, an' then the belts went whirraru!
I misremember what occurred, but subsequint the storm
A Freeman's Journal Supplemint was all my uniform.
    O it was: -- "Belts . . .

There was a row in Silver Street -- they sent the Polis there,
The English were too drunk to know, the Irish didn't care;
But when they grew impertinint we simultaneous rose,
Till half o' them was Liffey mud an' half was tatthered clo'es.
    For it was: -- "Belts . . .

There was a row in Silver Street -- it might ha' raged till now,
But some one drew his side-arm clear, an' nobody knew how;
'Twas Hogan took the point an' dropped; we saw the red blood run:
An' so we all was murderers that started out in fun.
    While it was: -- "Belts . . .

There was a row in Silver Street -- but that put down the shine,
Wid each man whisperin' to his next: "'Twas never work o' mine!"
We went away like beaten dogs, an' down the street we bore him,
The poor dumb corpse that couldn't tell the bhoys were sorry for him.
    When it was: -- "Belts . . .

There was a row in Silver Street -- it isn't over yet,
For half of us are under guard wid punishments to get;
'Tis all a merricle to me as in the Clink I lie:
There was a row in Silver Street -- begod, I wonder why!
    But it was: -- "Belts, belts, belts, an' that's one for you!"
    An' it was "Belts, belts, belts, an' that's done for you!"
    O buckle an' tongue
    Was the song that we sung
    From Harrison's down to the Park!

The Young British Soldier

When the 'arf-made recruity goes out to the East
'E acts like a babe an' 'e drinks like a beast,
An' 'e wonders because 'e is frequent deceased
   Ere 'e's fit for to serve as a soldier.
     Serve, serve, serve as a soldier,
     Serve, serve, serve as a soldier,
     Serve, serve, serve as a soldier,
      So-oldier of the Queen!

Now all you recruities what's drafted to-day,
You shut up your rag-box an' 'ark to my lay,
An' I'll sing you a soldier as far as I may:
   A soldier what's fit for a soldier.
    Fit, fit, fit for a soldier . . .

First mind you steer clear o' the grog-sellers' huts,
For they sell you Fixed Bay'nets that rots out your guts --
Ay, drink that 'ud eat the live steel from your butts --
   An' it's bad for the young British soldier.
    Bad, bad, bad for the soldier . . .

When the cholera comes -- as it will past a doubt --
Keep out of the wet and don't go on the shout,
For the sickness gets in as the liquor dies out,
   An' it crumples the young British soldier.
    Crum-, crum-, crumples the soldier . . .

But the worst o' your foes is the sun over'ead:
You must wear your 'elmet for all that is said:
If 'e finds you uncovered 'e'll knock you down dead,
   An' you'll die like a fool of a soldier.
    Fool, fool, fool of a soldier . . .

If you're cast for fatigue by a sergeant unkind,
Don't grouse like a woman nor crack on nor blind;
Be handy and civil, and then you will find
   That it's beer for the young British soldier.
    Beer, beer, beer for the soldier . . .

Now, if you must marry, take care she is old --
A troop-sergeant's widow's the nicest I'm told,
For beauty won't help if your rations is cold,
   Nor love ain't enough for a soldier.
    'Nough, 'nough, 'nough for a soldier . . .

If the wife should go wrong with a comrade, be loath
To shoot when you catch 'em -- you'll swing, on my oath! --
Make 'im take 'er and keep 'er: that's Hell for them both,
   An' you're shut o' the curse of a soldier.

Curse, curse, curse of a soldier . . .

When first under fire an' you're wishful to duck,
Don't look nor take 'eed at the man that is struck,
Be thankful you're livin', and trust to your luck
   And march to your front like a soldier.
      Front, front, front like a soldier . . .

When 'arf of your bullets fly wide in the ditch,
Don't call your Martini a cross-eyed old bitch;
She's human as you are -- you treat her as sich,
   An' she'll fight for the young British soldier.
      Fight, fight, fight for the soldier . . .

When shakin' their bustles like ladies so fine,
The guns o' the enemy wheel into line,
Shoot low at the limbers an' don't mind the shine,
   For noise never startles the soldier.
      Start-, start-, startles the soldier . . .

If your officer's dead and the sergeants look white,
Remember it's ruin to run from a fight:
So take open order, lie down, and sit tight,
   And wait for supports like a soldier.
      Wait, wait, wait like a soldier . . .

When you're wounded and left on Afghanistan's plains,
And the women come out to cut up what remains,
Jest roll to your rifle and blow out your brains

   An' go to your Gawd like a soldier.
     Go, go, go like a soldier,
     Go, go, go like a soldier,
     Go, go, go like a soldier,
      So-oldier of the Queen!

Mandalay

By the old Moulmein Pagoda, lookin' eastward to the sea,
There's a Burma girl a-settin', and I know she thinks o' me;
For the wind is in the palm-trees, and the temple-bells they say:
"Come you back, you British soldier; come you back to Mandalay!"
    Come you back to Mandalay,
    Where the old Flotilla lay:
    Can't you 'ear their paddles chunkin' from Rangoon to Mandalay?
On the road to Mandalay,
    Where the flyin'-fishes play,
    An' the dawn comes up like thunder outer China 'crost the Bay!

'Er petticoat was yaller an' 'er little cap was green,
An' 'er name was Supi-yaw-lat -- jes' the same as Theebaw's Queen,
An' I seed her first a-smokin' of a whackin' white cheroot,
An' a-wastin' Christian kisses on an 'eathen idol's foot:
    Bloomin' idol made o'mud --
    Wot they called the Great Gawd Budd --
    Plucky lot she cared for idols when I kissed 'er where she stud!
On the road to Mandalay . . .

When the mist was on the rice-fields an' the sun was droppin' slow,
She'd git 'er little banjo an' she'd sing "Kulla-lo-lo!"
With 'er arm upon my shoulder an' 'er cheek agin' my cheek
We useter watch the steamers an' the hathis pilin' teak.
    Elephints a-pilin' teak
    In the sludgy, squdgy creek,
    Where the silence 'ung that 'eavy you was 'arf afraid to speak!
On the road to Mandalay . . .

But that's all shove be'ind me -- long ago an' fur away,
An' there ain't no 'busses runnin' from the Bank to Mandalay;
An' I'm learnin' 'ere in London what the ten-year soldier tells:
"If you've 'eard the East a-callin', you won't never 'eed naught else."
    No! you won't 'eed nothin' else
    But them spicy garlic smells,
    An' the sunshine an' the palm-trees an' the tinkly temple-bells;
On the road to Mandalay . . .

I am sick o' wastin' leather on these gritty pavin'-stones,
An' the blasted Henglish drizzle wakes the fever in my bones;
Tho' I walks with fifty 'ousemaids outer Chelsea to the Strand,
An' they talks a lot o' lovin', but wot do they understand?
    Beefy face an' grubby 'and --
    Law! wot do they understand?
    I've a neater, sweeter maiden in a cleaner, greener land!
On the road to Mandalay . . .

Ship me somewheres east of Suez, where the best is like the worst,
Where there aren't no Ten Commandments an' a man can raise a thirst;

For the temple-bells are callin', an' it's there that I would be --
By the old Moulmein Pagoda, looking lazy at the sea;
    On the road to Mandalay,
    Where the old Flotilla lay,
    With our sick beneath the awnings when we went to Mandalay!
    On the road to Mandalay,
    Where the flyin'-fishes play,
    An' the dawn comes up like thunder outer China 'crost the Bay!

Troopin'

(Our Army in the East)

Troopin', troopin', troopin' to the sea:
'Ere's September come again -- the six-year men are free.
O leave the dead be'ind us, for they cannot come away
To where the ship's a-coalin' up that takes us 'ome to-day.
  We're goin' 'ome, we're goin' 'ome,
   Our ship is at the shore,
  An' you must pack your 'aversack,
   For we won't come back no more.
  Ho, don't you grieve for me,
   My lovely Mary-Ann,
  For I'll marry you yit on a fourp'ny bit
   As a time-expired man.

The Malabar's in 'arbour with the Jumner at 'er tail,
An' the time-expired's waitin' of 'is orders for to sail.
Ho! the weary waitin' when on Khyber 'ills we lay,
But the time-expired's waitin' of 'is orders 'ome to-day.

They'll turn us out at Portsmouth wharf in cold an' wet an' rain,
All wearin' Injian cotton kit, but we will not complain;
They'll kill us of pneumonia -- for that's their little way --
But damn the chills and fever, men, we're goin' 'ome to-day!

Troopin', troopin', winter's round again!
See the new draf's pourin' in for the old campaign;
Ho, you poor recruities, but you've got to earn your pay --
What's the last from Lunnon, lads? We're goin' there to-day.

Troopin', troopin', give another cheer --
'Ere's to English women an' a quart of English beer.
The Colonel an' the regiment an' all who've got to stay,
Gawd's mercy strike 'em gentle -- Whoop! we're goin' 'ome to-day.
  We're goin' 'ome, we're goin' 'ome,
   Our ship is at the shore,
  An' you must pack your 'aversack,
   For we won't come back no more.
  Ho, don't you grieve for me,
   My lovely Mary-Ann,
  For I'll marry you yit on a fourp'ny bit
   As a time-expired man.

The Widow's Party

"Where have you been this while away,
    Johnnie, Johnnie?"
'Long with the rest on a picnic lay,
    Johnnie, my Johnnie, aha!
They called us out of the barrack-yard
To Gawd knows where from Gosport Hard,
And you can't refuse when you get the card,
    And the Widow gives the party.
        (Bugle: Ta--rara--ra-ra-rara!)

"What did you get to eat and drink,
    Johnnie, Johnnie?"
Standing water as thick as ink,
    Johnnie, my Johnnie, aha!
A bit o' beef that were three year stored,
A bit o' mutton as tough as a board,
And a fowl we killed with a sergeant's sword,
    When the Widow give the party.

"What did you do for knives and forks,
    Johnnie, Johnnie?"
We carries 'em with us wherever we walks,
    Johnnie, my Johnnie, aha!
And some was sliced and some was halved,
And some was crimped and some was carved,
And some was gutted and some was starved,
    When the Widow give the party.

"What ha' you done with half your mess,
    Johnnie, Johnnie?"
They couldn't do more and they wouldn't do less,
    Johnnie, my Johnnie, aha!
They ate their whack and they drank their fill,
And I think the rations has made them ill,
For half my comp'ny's lying still
    Where the Widow give the party.

"How did you get away -- away,
    Johnnie, Johnnie?"
On the broad o' my back at the end o' the day,
    Johnnie, my Johnnie, aha!
I comed away like a bleedin' toff,
For I got four niggers to carry me off,
As I lay in the bight of a canvas trough,
    When the Widow give the party.

"What was the end of all the show,
    Johnnie, Johnnie?"
Ask my Colonel, for I don't know,

Johnnie, my Johnnie, aha!
We broke a King and we built a road --
A court-house stands where the reg'ment goed.
And the river's clean where the raw blood flowed
When the Widow give the party.
(Bugle: Ta--rara--ra-ra-rara!)

Ford o' Kabul River

Kabul town's by Kabul river --
 Blow the bugle, draw the sword --
There I lef' my mate for ever,
 Wet an' drippin' by the ford.
   Ford, ford, ford o' Kabul river,
   Ford o' Kabul river in the dark!
   There's the river up and brimmin', an' there's 'arf a squadron swimmin'
   'Cross the ford o' Kabul river in the dark.

Kabul town's a blasted place --
 Blow the bugle, draw the sword --
'Strewth I sha'n't forget 'is face
 Wet an' drippin' by the ford!
   Ford, ford, ford o' Kabul river,
   Ford o' Kabul river in the dark!
   Keep the crossing-stakes beside you, an' they will surely guide you
   'Cross the ford o' Kabul river in the dark.

Kabul town is sun and dust --
 Blow the bugle, draw the sword --
I'd ha' sooner drownded fust
 'Stead of 'im beside the ford.
   Ford, ford, ford o' Kabul river,
   Ford o' Kabul river in the dark!
   You can 'ear the 'orses threshin', you can 'ear the men a-splashin',
   'Cross the ford o' Kabul river in the dark.

Kabul town was ours to take --
 Blow the bugle, draw the sword --
I'd ha' left it for 'is sake --
 'Im that left me by the ford.
   Ford, ford, ford o' Kabul river,
   Ford o' Kabul river in the dark!
   It's none so bloomin' dry there; ain't you never comin' nigh there,
   'Cross the ford o' Kabul river in the dark?

Kabul town'll go to hell --
 Blow the bugle, draw the sword --
'Fore I see him 'live an' well --
 'Im the best beside the ford.
   Ford, ford, ford o' Kabul river,
   Ford o' Kabul river in the dark!
   Gawd 'elp 'em if they blunder, for their boots'll pull 'em under,
   By the ford o' Kabul river in the dark.

Turn your 'orse from Kabul town --
 Blow the bugle, draw the sword --
'Im an' 'arf my troop is down,
 Down an' drownded by the ford.

Ford, ford, ford o' Kabul river,
 Ford o' Kabul river in the dark!
There's the river low an' fallin', but it ain't no use o' callin'
 'Cross the ford o' Kabul river in the dark.

Gentlemen-Rankers

To the legion of the lost ones, to the cohort of the damned,
  To my brethren in their sorrow overseas,
Sings a gentleman of England cleanly bred, machinely crammed,
  And a trooper of the Empress, if you please.
Yea, a trooper of the forces who has run his own six horses,
  And faith he went the pace and went it blind,
And the world was more than kin while he held the ready tin,
  But to-day the Sergeant's something less than kind.
    We're poor little lambs who've lost our way,
      Baa! Baa! Baa!
    We're little black sheep who've gone astray,
      Baa--aa--aa!
    Gentlemen-rankers out on the spree,
    Damned from here to Eternity,
    God ha' mercy on such as we,
      Baa! Yah! Bah!

Oh, it's sweet to sweat through stables, sweet to empty kitchen slops,
  And it's sweet to hear the tales the troopers tell,
To dance with blowzy housemaids at the regimental hops
  And thrash the cad who says you waltz too well.
Yes, it makes you cock-a-hoop to be "Rider" to your troop,
  And branded with a blasted worsted spur,
When you envy, O how keenly, one poor Tommy being cleanly
  Who blacks your boots and sometimes calls you "Sir".

If the home we never write to, and the oaths we never keep,
  And all we know most distant and most dear,
Across the snoring barrack-room return to break our sleep,
  Can you blame us if we soak ourselves in beer?
When the drunken comrade mutters and the great guard-lantern gutters
  And the horror of our fall is written plain,
Every secret, self-revealing on the aching white-washed ceiling,
  Do you wonder that we drug ourselves from pain?

We have done with Hope and Honour, we are lost to Love and Truth,
  We are dropping down the ladder rung by rung,
And the measure of our torment is the measure of our youth.
  God help us, for we knew the worst too young!
Our shame is clean repentance for the crime that brought the sentence,
  Our pride it is to know no spur of pride,
And the Curse of Reuben holds us till an alien turf enfolds us
  And we die, and none can tell Them where we died.
    We're poor little lambs who've lost our way,
      Baa! Baa! Baa!
    We're little black sheep who've gone astray,
      Baa--aa--aa!
    Gentlemen-rankers out on the spree,
    Damned from here to Eternity,

God ha' mercy on such as we,
  Baa! Yah! Bah!

Route Marchin'

We're marchin' on relief over Injia's sunny plains,
A little front o' Christmas-time an' just be'ind the Rains;
Ho! get away you bullock-man, you've 'eard the bugle blowed,
There's a regiment a-comin' down the Grand Trunk Road;
    With its best foot first
    And the road a-sliding past,
    An' every bloomin' campin'-ground exactly like the last;
    While the Big Drum says,
    With 'is "rowdy-dowdy-dow!" --
    "Kiko kissywarsti don't you hamsher argy jow?"
Oh, there's them Injian temples to admire when you see,
There's the peacock round the corner an' the monkey up the tree,
An' there's that rummy silver grass a-wavin' in the wind,
An' the old Grand Trunk a-trailin' like a rifle-sling be'ind.
    While it's best foot first, . . .

At half-past five's Revelly, an' our tents they down must come,
Like a lot of button mushrooms when you pick 'em up at 'ome.
But it's over in a minute, an' at six the column starts,
While the women and the kiddies sit an' shiver in the carts.
    An' it's best foot first, . . .

Oh, then it's open order, an' we lights our pipes an' sings,
An' we talks about our rations an' a lot of other things,
An' we thinks o' friends in England, an' we wonders what they're at,
An' 'ow they would admire for to hear us sling the bat.
    An' it's best foot first, . . .
It's none so bad o' Sunday, when you're lyin' at your ease,
To watch the kites a-wheelin' round them feather-'eaded trees,
For although there ain't no women, yet there ain't no barrick-yards,
So the orficers goes shootin' an' the men they plays at cards.
    Till it's best foot first, . . .

So 'ark an' 'eed, you rookies, which is always grumblin' sore,
There's worser things than marchin' from Umballa to Cawnpore;
An' if your 'eels are blistered an' they feels to 'urt like 'ell,
You drop some tallow in your socks an' that will make 'em well.
    For it's best foot first, . . .

We're marchin' on relief over Injia's coral strand,
Eight 'undred fightin' Englishmen, the Colonel, and the Band;
Ho! get away you bullock-man, you've 'eard the bugle blowed,
There's a regiment a-comin' down the Grand Trunk Road;
    With its best foot first
    And the road a-sliding past,
    An' every bloomin' campin'-ground exactly like the last;
    While the Big Drum says,
    With 'is "rowdy-dowdy-dow!" --
    "Kiko kissywarsti don't you hamsher argy jow?"

Shillin' a Day

My name is O'Kelly, I've heard the Revelly
From Birr to Bareilly, from Leeds to Lahore,
Hong-Kong and Peshawur,
Lucknow and Etawah,
And fifty-five more all endin' in "pore".
Black Death and his quickness, the depth and the thickness,
Of sorrow and sickness I've known on my way,
But I'm old and I'm nervis,
I'm cast from the Service,
And all I deserve is a shillin' a day.
 (Chorus) Shillin' a day,
        Bloomin' good pay --
        Lucky to touch it, a shillin' a day!

Oh, it drives me half crazy to think of the days I
Went slap for the Ghazi, my sword at my side,
When we rode Hell-for-leather
Both squadrons together,
That didn't care whether we lived or we died.
But it's no use despairin', my wife must go charin'
An' me commissairin' the pay-bills to better,
So if me you be'old
In the wet and the cold,
By the Grand Metropold, won't you give me a letter?
 (Full chorus) Give 'im a letter --
        'Can't do no better,
        Late Troop-Sergeant-Major an' -- runs with a letter!
        Think what 'e's been,
        Think what 'e's seen,
        Think of his pension an' ----

        Gawd save the Queen

SECOND SERIES (1896)

'Bobs'

There's a little red-faced man,
    Which is Bobs,
Rides the tallest 'orse 'e can-
    Our Bobs,
If it bucks or kicks or rears,
'E can sit for twenty years
With a smile round both 'is ears-
    Can't yer, Bobs?

Then 'ere's to Bobs Bahadur-
    Little Bobs, Bobs, Bobs!
'E's or pukka Kandaharder-
    Fightin' Bobs, Bobs, Bobs!
'E's the Dook of Aggy Chel;
'E's the man that done us well,
An' we'll follow 'im to 'ell-
    Won't we Bobs?

If a limber's slipped a trace,
    'Ook on Bobs.
If a marker's lost 'is place,
    Dress by Bobs.
For 'e's eyes all up 'is coat,
An' a bugle in 'is throat,
An' you will not play the goat
    Under Bobs.

'E's a little down on drink,
    Chaplain Bobs;
But it keeps us outer Clink-
    Don't it Bobs?
So we will not complain
Tho' 'e's water on the brain,
If 'e leads us straight again-
    Blue-light Bobs.

If you stood 'im on 'is head
    Father Bobs,
You could spill a quart o' lead
    Outer Bobs.
'E's been at it thirty years,
An' amassin souveneers
In the way o' slugs an' spears-

Ain't yer, Bobs?

What 'e does not Know o' war,
    Gen'ral Bobs,
You can arst the shop next door-
    Can't they, Bobs?
Oh, 'e's little, but he's wise;
'E's a terror for 'is size,
An'-'e-does-not-advertise-
    Do yer, Bobs?

Now they've made a bloomin' Lord
    Outer Bobs,
Which was but 'is fair reward-
    Weren't it Bobs?
So 'e'll wear a coronet
Where 'is 'elmet used to set;
But we know you won't forget-
    Will yer, Bobs?

Then 'ere's to Bobs Bahadur-
    Little Bobs, Bobs, Bobs!
Pocket-Wellin'ton an' arder -
    Fightin' Bobs, Bobs, Bobs!
This ain't no bloomin' ode,
But you've 'elped the soldier's load,
An' for benefits bestowed,
    Bless yer, Bobs!

'Back to the Army Again'

I'm 'ere in a ticky ulster an' a broken billycock 'at,
A-layin' on to the sergeant I don't know a gun from a bat;
My shirt's doin' duty for jacket, my sock's stickin' out o' my boots,
An' I'm learnin' the damned old goose-step along o' the new recruits!

   Back to the Army again, sergeant,
    Back to the Army again.
   Don't look so 'ard, for I 'aven't no card,
    I'm back to the Army again!

I done my six years' service. 'Er Majesty sez: "Good-day --
You'll please to come when you're rung for, an' 'ere's your 'ole back-pay;
An' fourpence a day for baccy -- an' bloomin' gen'rous, too;
An' now you can make your fortune -- the same as your orf'cers do."

   Back to the Army again, sergeant,
    Back to the Army again;
   'Ow did I learn to do right-about turn?
    I'm back to the Army again!

A man o' four-an'-twenty that 'asn't learned of a trade --
Beside "Reserve" agin' him -- 'e'd better be never made.
I tried my luck for a quarter, an' that was enough for me,
An' I thought of 'Er Majesty's barricks, an' I thought I'd go an' see.

   Back to the Army again, sergeant,
    Back to the Army again;
   'Tisn't my fault if I dress when I 'alt --
    I'm back to the Army again!

The sergeant arst no questions, but 'e winked the other eye,
'E sez to me, "'Shun!" an' I shunted, the same as in days gone by;
For 'e saw the set o' my shoulders, an' I couldn't 'elp 'oldin' straight
When me an' the other rookies come under the barrick-gate.

   Back to the Army again, sergeant,
    Back to the Army again;
   'Oo would ha' thought I could carry an' port?
    I'm back to the Army again!

I took my bath, an' I wallered -- for, Gawd, I needed it so!
I smelt the smell o' the barricks, I 'eard the bugles go.
I 'eard the feet on the gravel -- the feet o' the men what drill --
An' I sez to my flutterin' 'eart-strings, I sez to 'em, "Peace, be still!"

   Back to the Army again, sergeant,
    Back to the Army again;
   'Oo said I knew when the Jumner was due?
    I'm back to the Army again!

I carried my slops to the tailor; I sez to 'im, "None o' your lip!
You tight 'em over the shoulders, an' loose 'em over the 'ip,
For the set o' the tunic's 'orrid." An' 'e sez to me, "Strike me dead,
But I thought you was used to the business!" an' so 'e done what I said.

   Back to the Army again, sergeant,
    Back to the Army again.
   Rather too free with my fancies? Wot -- me?
    I'm back to the Army again!

Next week I'll 'ave 'em fitted; I'll buy me a swagger-cane;
They'll let me free o' the barricks to walk on the Hoe again
In the name o' William Parsons, that used to be Edward Clay,
An' -- any pore beggar that wants it can draw my fourpence a day!

   Back to the Army again, sergeant,
    Back to the Army again:
   Out o' the cold an' the rain, sergeant,
    Out o' the cold an' the rain.

      'Oo's there?
A man that's too good to be lost you,
 A man that is 'andled an' made --
A man that will pay what 'e cost you
 In learnin' the others their trade -- parade!
You're droppin' the pick o' the Army
 Because you don't 'elp 'em remain,
But drives 'em to cheat to get out o' the street
 An' back to the Army again!

'Birds of Prey' March

March! The mud is cakin' good about our trousies.
 Front! -- eyes front, an' watch the Colour-casin's drip.
Front! The faces of the women in the 'ouses
 Ain't the kind o' things to take aboard the ship.

    Cheer! An' we'll never march to victory.
    Cheer! An' we'll never live to 'ear the cannon roar!
      The Large Birds o' Prey
      They will carry us away,
    An' you'll never see your soldiers any more!

Wheel! Oh, keep your touch; we're goin' round a corner.
 Time! -- mark time, an' let the men be'ind us close.
Lord! the transport's full, an' 'alf our lot not on 'er --
 Cheer, O cheer! We're going off where no one knows.

March! The Devil's none so black as 'e is painted!
 Cheer! We'll 'ave some fun before we're put away.
'Alt, an' 'and 'er out -- a woman's gone and fainted!
 Cheer! Get on -- Gawd 'elp the married men to-day!

Hoi! Come up, you 'ungry beggars, to yer sorrow.
 ('Ear them say they want their tea, an' want it quick!)
You won't have no mind for slingers, not to-morrow --
 No; you'll put the 'tween-decks stove out, bein' sick!

'Alt! The married kit 'as all to go before us!
 'Course it's blocked the bloomin' gangway up again!
Cheer, O cheer the 'Orse Guards watchin' tender o'er us,
 Keepin' us since eight this mornin' in the rain!

Stuck in 'eavy marchin'-order, sopped and wringin' --
 Sick, before our time to watch 'er 'eave an' fall,
'Ere's your 'appy 'ome at last, an' stop your singin'.
 'Alt! Fall in along the troop-deck! Silence all!

    Cheer! For we'll never live to see no bloomin' victory!
    Cheer! An' we'll never live to 'ear the cannon roar! (One cheer more!)
      The jackal an' the kite
      'Ave an 'ealthy appetite,
    An' you'll never see your soldiers any more! ('Ip! Urroar!)
      The eagle an' the crow
      They are waitin' ever so,
    An' you'll never see your soldiers any more! ('Ip! Urroar!)
      Yes, the Large Birds o' Prey
      They will carry us away,
    An' you'll never see your soldiers any more!

'Soldier an' Salor Too'

As I was spittin' into the Ditch aboard o' the Crocodile,
I seed a man on a man-o'-war got up in the Reg'lars' style.
'E was scrapin' the paint from off of 'er plates,
  an' I sez to 'im, "'Oo are you?"
Sez 'e, "I'm a Jolly -- 'Er Majesty's Jolly -- soldier an' sailor too!"
Now 'is work begins by Gawd knows when, and 'is work is never through;
'E isn't one o' the reg'lar Line, nor 'e isn't one of the crew.
'E's a kind of a giddy harumfrodite -- soldier an' sailor too!

An' after I met 'im all over the world, a-doin' all kinds of things,
Like landin' 'isself with a Gatlin' gun to talk to them 'eathen kings;
'E sleeps in an 'ammick instead of a cot,
  an' 'e drills with the deck on a slew,
An' 'e sweats like a Jolly -- 'Er Majesty's Jolly -- soldier an' sailor too!
For there isn't a job on the top o' the earth the beggar don't know, nor do --
You can leave 'im at night on a bald man's 'ead, to paddle 'is own canoe --
'E's a sort of a bloomin' cosmopolouse -- soldier an' sailor too.

We've fought 'em in trooper, we've fought 'em in dock,
  and drunk with 'em in betweens,
When they called us the seasick scull'ry-maids,
  an' we called 'em the Ass Marines;
But, when we was down for a double fatigue, from Woolwich to Bernardmyo,
We sent for the Jollies -- 'Er Majesty's Jollies -- soldier an' sailor too!
They think for 'emselves, an' they steal for 'emselves,
  and they never ask what's to do,
But they're camped an' fed an' they're up an' fed before our bugle's blew.
Ho! they ain't no limpin' procrastitutes -- soldier an' sailor too.

You may say we are fond of an 'arness-cut, or 'ootin' in barrick-yards,
Or startin' a Board School mutiny along o' the Onion Guards;
But once in a while we can finish in style for the ends of the earth to view,
The same as the Jollies -- 'Er Majesty's Jollies -- soldier an' sailor too!
They come of our lot, they was brothers to us;
  they was beggars we'd met an' knew;
Yes, barrin' an inch in the chest an' the arm, they was doubles o' me an' you;
For they weren't no special chrysanthemums -- soldier an' sailor too!

To take your chance in the thick of a rush, with firing all about,
Is nothing so bad when you've cover to 'and, an' leave an' likin' to shout;
But to stand an' be still to the Birken'ead drill
  is a damn tough bullet to chew,
An' they done it, the Jollies -- 'Er Majesty's Jollies --
  soldier an' sailor too!
Their work was done when it 'adn't begun; they was younger nor me an' you;
Their choice it was plain between drownin' in 'eaps
  an' bein' mopped by the screw,
So they stood an' was still to the Birken'ead drill, soldier an' sailor too!

We're most of us liars, we're 'arf of us thieves,
  an' the rest are as rank as can be,
But once in a while we can finish in style
  (which I 'ope it won't 'appen to me).
But it makes you think better o' you an' your friends,
  an' the work you may 'ave to do,
When you think o' the sinkin' Victorier's Jollies -- soldier an' sailor too!
Now there isn't no room for to say ye don't know --
  they 'ave proved it plain and true --
That whether it's Widow, or whether it's ship, Victorier's work is to do,
An' they done it, the Jollies -- 'Er Majesty's Jollies --
  soldier an' sailor too!

Sappers

When the Waters were dried an' the Earth did appear,
 ("It's all one," says the Sapper),
The Lord He created the Engineer,
 Her Majesty's Royal Engineer,
 With the rank and pay of a Sapper!

When the Flood come along for an extra monsoon,
'Twas Noah constructed the first pontoon
 To the plans of Her Majesty's, etc.

But after fatigue in the wet an' the sun,
Old Noah got drunk, which he wouldn't ha' done
 If he'd trained with, etc.

When the Tower o' Babel had mixed up men's bat,
Some clever civilian was managing that,
 An' none of, etc.

When the Jews had a fight at the foot of a hill,
Young Joshua ordered the sun to stand still,
 For he was a Captain of Engineers, etc.

When the Children of Israel made bricks without straw,
They were learnin' the regular work of our Corps,
 The work of, etc.

For ever since then, if a war they would wage,
Behold us a-shinin' on history's page --
 First page for, etc.

We lay down their sidings an' help 'em entrain,
An' we sweep up their mess through the bloomin' campaign,
 In the style of, etc.

They send us in front with a fuse an' a mine
To blow up the gates that are rushed by the Line,
 But bent by, etc.

They send us behind with a pick an' a spade,
To dig for the guns of a bullock-brigade
 Which has asked for, etc.

We work under escort in trousers and shirt,
An' the heathen they plug us tail-up in the dirt,
 Annoying, etc.

We blast out the rock an' we shovel the mud,
We make 'em good roads an' -- they roll down the khud,
 Reporting, etc.

We make 'em their bridges, their wells, an' their huts,
An' the telegraph-wire the enemy cuts,
  An' it's blamed on, etc.

An' when we return, an' from war we would cease,
They grudge us adornin' the billets of peace,
  Which are kept for, etc.

We build 'em nice barracks -- they swear they are bad,
That our Colonels are Methodist, married or mad,
  Insultin', etc.

They haven't no manners nor gratitude too,
For the more that we help 'em, the less will they do,
  But mock at, etc.

Now the Line's but a man with a gun in his hand,
An' Cavalry's only what horses can stand,
  When helped by, etc.

Artillery moves by the leave o' the ground,
But we are the men that do something all round,
  For we are, etc.

I have stated it plain, an' my argument's thus
  ("It's all one," says the Sapper),
There's only one Corps which is perfect -- that's us;
  An' they call us Her Majesty's Engineers,
  Her Majesty's Royal Engineers,
  With the rank and pay of a Sapper!

That Day

It got beyond all orders an' it got beyond all 'ope;
 It got to shammin' wounded an' retirin' from the 'alt.
'Ole companies was lookin' for the nearest road to slope;
 It were just a bloomin' knock-out -- an' our fault!

  Now there ain't no chorus 'ere to give,
   Nor there ain't no band to play;
  An' I wish I was dead 'fore I done what I did,
   Or seen what I seed that day!

We was sick o' bein' punished, an' we let 'em know it, too;
 An' a company-commander up an' 'it us with a sword,
An' some one shouted "'Ook it!" an' it come to sove-ki-poo,
 An' we chucked our rifles from us -- O my Gawd!

There was thirty dead an' wounded on the ground we wouldn't keep --
 No, there wasn't more than twenty when the front begun to go;
But, Christ! along the line o' flight they cut us up like sheep,
 An' that was all we gained by doin' so.

I 'eard the knives be'ind me, but I dursn't face my man,
 Nor I don't know where I went to, 'cause I didn't 'alt to see,
Till I 'eard a beggar squealin' out for quarter as 'e ran,
 An' I thought I knew the voice an' -- it was me!

We was 'idin' under bedsteads more than 'arf a march away;
 We was lyin' up like rabbits all about the countryside;
An' the major cursed 'is Maker 'cause 'e lived to see that day,
 An' the colonel broke 'is sword acrost, an' cried.

We was rotten 'fore we started -- we was never disciplined;
 We made it out a favour if an order was obeyed;
Yes, every little drummer 'ad 'is rights an' wrongs to mind,
 So we had to pay for teachin' -- an' we paid!

The papers 'id it 'andsome, but you know the Army knows;
 We was put to groomin' camels till the regiments withdrew,
An' they gave us each a medal for subduin' England's foes,
 An' I 'ope you like my song -- because it's true!

  An' there ain't no chorus 'ere to give,
   Nor there ain't no band to play;
  But I wish I was dead 'fore I done what I did,
   Or seen what I seed that day!

'The Men that fought at Minden'

A Song of Instruction

The men that fought at Minden, they was rookies in their time --
  So was them that fought at Waterloo!
All the 'ole command, yuss, from Minden to Maiwand,
  They was once dam' sweeps like you!

   Then do not be discouraged, 'Eaven is your 'elper,
    We'll learn you not to forget;
    An' you mustn't swear an' curse, or you'll only catch it worse,
    For we'll make you soldiers yet!

The men that fought at Minden, they 'ad stocks beneath their chins,
  Six inch 'igh an' more;
But fatigue it was their pride, and they would not be denied
  To clean the cook-'ouse floor.

The men that fought at Minden, they had anarchistic bombs
  Served to 'em by name of 'and-grenades;
But they got it in the eye (same as you will by-an'-by)
  When they clubbed their field-parades.

The men that fought at Minden, they 'ad buttons up an' down,
  Two-an'-twenty dozen of 'em told;
But they didn't grouse an' shirk at an hour's extry work,
  They kept 'em bright as gold.

The men that fought at Minden, they was armed with musketoons,
  Also, they was drilled by 'alberdiers;
I don't know what they were, but the sergeants took good care
  They washed be'ind their ears.

The men that fought at Minden, they 'ad ever cash in 'and
  Which they did not bank nor save,
But spent it gay an' free on their betters -- such as me --
  For the good advice I gave.

The men that fought at Minden, they was civil -- yuss, they was --
  Never didn't talk o' rights an' wrongs,
But they got it with the toe (same as you will get it -- so!) --
  For interrupting songs.

The men that fought at Minden, they was several other things
  Which I don't remember clear;
But that's the reason why, now the six-year men are dry,
  The rooks will stand the beer!

   Then do not be discouraged, 'Eaven is your 'elper,
    We'll learn you not to forget;

An' you mustn't swear an' curse, or you'll only catch it worse,
 For we'll make you soldiers yet!

Soldiers yet, if you've got it in you --
 All for the sake of the Core;
Soldiers yet, if we 'ave to skin you --
 Run an' get the beer, Johnny Raw -- Johnny Raw!
 Ho! run an' get the beer, Johnny Raw!

Cholera Camp

We've got the cholerer in camp -- it's worse than forty fights;
 We're dyin' in the wilderness the same as Isrulites;
It's before us, an' be'ind us, an' we cannot get away,
 An' the doctor's just reported we've ten more to-day!

  Oh, strike your camp an' go, the Bugle's callin',
    The Rains are fallin' --
  The dead are bushed an' stoned to keep 'em safe below;
  The Band's a-doin' all she knows to cheer us;
  The Chaplain's gone and prayed to Gawd to 'ear us --
    To 'ear us --
  O Lord, for it's a-killin' of us so!

Since August, when it started, it's been stickin' to our tail,
Though they've 'ad us out by marches an' they've 'ad us back by rail;
But it runs as fast as troop-trains, and we cannot get away;
An' the sick-list to the Colonel makes ten more to-day.

There ain't no fun in women nor there ain't no bite to drink;
It's much too wet for shootin', we can only march and think;
An' at evenin', down the nullahs, we can 'ear the jackals say,
"Get up, you rotten beggars, you've ten more to-day!"

'Twould make a monkey cough to see our way o' doin' things --
Lieutenants takin' companies an' captains takin' wings,
An' Lances actin' Sergeants -- eight file to obey --
For we've lots o' quick promotion on ten deaths a day!

Our Colonel's white an' twitterly -- 'e gets no sleep nor food,
But mucks about in 'orspital where nothing does no good.
'E sends us 'eaps o' comforts, all bought from 'is pay --
But there aren't much comfort 'andy on ten deaths a day.

Our Chaplain's got a banjo, an' a skinny mule 'e rides,
An' the stuff 'e says an' sings us, Lord, it makes us split our sides!
With 'is black coat-tails a-bobbin' to Ta-ra-ra Boom-der-ay!
'E's the proper kind o' padre for ten deaths a day.

An' Father Victor 'elps 'im with our Roman Catholicks --
He knows an 'eap of Irish songs an' rummy conjurin' tricks;
An' the two they works together when it comes to play or pray;
So we keep the ball a-rollin' on ten deaths a day.

We've got the cholerer in camp -- we've got it 'ot an' sweet;
It ain't no Christmas dinner, but it's 'elped an' we must eat.
We've gone beyond the funkin', 'cause we've found it doesn't pay,
An' we're rockin' round the Districk on ten deaths a day!

  Then strike your camp an' go, the Rains are fallin',

The Bugle's callin'!
The dead are bushed an' stoned to keep 'em safe below!
An' them that do not like it they can lump it,
An' them that cannot stand it they can jump it;
We've got to die somewhere -- some way -- some'ow --
We might as well begin to do it now!
Then, Number One, let down the tent-pole slow,
Knock out the pegs an' 'old the corners -- so!
Fold in the flies, furl up the ropes, an' stow!
Oh, strike -- oh, strike your camp an' go!
    (Gawd 'elp us!)

The Ladies

I've taken my fun where I've found it;
 I've rogued an' I've ranged in my time;
I've 'ad my pickin' o' sweet'earts,
 An' four o' the lot was prime.
One was an 'arf-caste widow,
 One was a woman at Prome,
One was the wife of a jemadar-sais,
 An' one is a girl at 'ome.

   Now I aren't no 'and with the ladies,
    For, takin' 'em all along,
   You never can say till you've tried 'em,
    An' then you are like to be wrong.
   There's times when you'll think that you mightn't,
    There's times when you'll know that you might;
   But the things you will learn from the Yellow an' Brown,
    They'll 'elp you a lot with the White!

I was a young un at 'Oogli,
 Shy as a girl to begin;
Aggie de Castrer she made me,
 An' Aggie was clever as sin;
Older than me, but my first un --
 More like a mother she were --
Showed me the way to promotion an' pay,
 An' I learned about women from 'er!

Then I was ordered to Burma,
 Actin' in charge o' Bazar,
An' I got me a tiddy live 'eathen
 Through buyin' supplies off 'er pa.
Funny an' yellow an' faithful --
 Doll in a teacup she were,
But we lived on the square, like a true-married pair,
 An' I learned about women from 'er!

Then we was shifted to Neemuch
 (Or I might ha' been keepin' 'er now),
An' I took with a shiny she-devil,
 The wife of a nigger at Mhow;
'Taught me the gipsy-folks' bolee;
 Kind o' volcano she were,
For she knifed me one night 'cause I wished she was white,
 And I learned about women from 'er!

Then I come 'ome in the trooper,
 'Long of a kid o' sixteen --
Girl from a convent at Meerut,
 The straightest I ever 'ave seen.

Love at first sight was 'er trouble,
 She didn't know what it were;
An' I wouldn't do such, 'cause I liked 'er too much,
 But -- I learned about women from 'er!

I've taken my fun where I've found it,
 An' now I must pay for my fun,
For the more you 'ave known o' the others
 The less will you settle to one;
An' the end of it's sittin' and thinkin',
 An' dreamin' Hell-fires to see;
So be warned by my lot (which I know you will not),
 An' learn about women from me!

   What did the Colonel's Lady think?
    Nobody never knew.
   Somebody asked the Sergeant's wife,
    An' she told 'em true!
   When you get to a man in the case,
    They're like as a row of pins --
   For the Colonel's Lady an' Judy O'Grady
    Are sisters under their skins!

Bill 'Awkins

"'As anybody seen Bill 'Awkins?"
  "Now 'ow in the devil would I know?"
"'E's taken my girl out walkin',
    An' I've got to tell 'im so --
      Gawd -- bless -- 'im!
    I've got to tell 'im so."

 "D'yer know what 'e's like, Bill 'Awkins?"
   "Now what in the devil would I care?"
"'E's the livin', breathin' image of an organ-grinder's monkey,
    With a pound of grease in 'is 'air --
      Gawd -- bless -- 'im!
    An' a pound o' grease in 'is 'air."

 "An' s'pose you met Bill 'Awkins,
   Now what in the devil 'ud ye do?"
"I'd open 'is cheek to 'is chin-strap buckle,
    An' bung up 'is both eyes, too --
      Gawd -- bless -- 'im!
    An' bung up 'is both eyes, too!"

 "Look 'ere, where 'e comes, Bill 'Awkins!
   Now what in the devil will you say?"
"It isn't fit an' proper to be fightin' on a Sunday,
    So I'll pass 'im the time o' day --
      Gawd -- bless -- 'im!
    I'll pass 'im the time o' day!"

The Mother-Lodge

There was Rundle, Station Master,
 An' Beazeley of the Rail,
An' 'Ackman, Commissariat,
 An' Donkin' o' the Jail;
An' Blake, Conductor-Sargent,
 Our Master twice was 'e,
With 'im that kept the Europe-shop,
 Old Framjee Eduljee.

    Outside -- "Sergeant! Sir! Salute! Salaam!"
    Inside -- "Brother", an' it doesn't do no 'arm.
    We met upon the Level an' we parted on the Square,
    An' I was Junior Deacon in my Mother-Lodge out there!

We'd Bola Nath, Accountant,
 An' Saul the Aden Jew,
An' Din Mohammed, draughtsman
 Of the Survey Office too;
There was Babu Chuckerbutty,
 An' Amir Singh the Sikh,
An' Castro from the fittin'-sheds,
 The Roman Catholick!

We 'adn't good regalia,
 An' our Lodge was old an' bare,
But we knew the Ancient Landmarks,
 An' we kep' 'em to a hair;
An' lookin' on it backwards
 It often strikes me thus,
There ain't such things as infidels,
 Excep', per'aps, it's us.

For monthly, after Labour,
 We'd all sit down and smoke
(We dursn't give no banquits,
 Lest a Brother's caste were broke),
An' man on man got talkin'
 Religion an' the rest,
An' every man comparin'
 Of the God 'e knew the best.

So man on man got talkin',
 An' not a Brother stirred
Till mornin' waked the parrots
 An' that dam' brain-fever-bird;
We'd say 'twas 'ighly curious,
 An' we'd all ride 'ome to bed,
With Mo'ammed, God, an' Shiva
 Changin' pickets in our 'ead.

Full oft on Guv'ment service
 This rovin' foot 'ath pressed,
An' bore fraternal greetin's
 To the Lodges east an' west,
Accordin' as commanded
 From Kohat to Singapore,
But I wish that I might see them
 In my Mother-Lodge once more!

I wish that I might see them,
 My Brethren black an' brown,
With the trichies smellin' pleasant
 An' the hog-darn passin' down;
An' the old khansamah snorin'
 On the bottle-khana floor,
Like a Master in good standing
 With my Mother-Lodge once more!

  Outside -- "Sergeant! Sir! Salute! Salaam!"
  Inside -- "Brother", an' it doesn't do no 'arm.
  We met upon the Level an' we parted on the Square,
  An' I was Junior Deacon in my Mother-Lodge out there!

'Follow Me 'Ome'

There was no one like 'im, 'Orse or Foot,
  Nor any o' the Guns I knew;
An' because it was so, why, o' course 'e went an' died,
  Which is just what the best men do.

  So it's knock out your pipes an' follow me!
  An' it's finish up your swipes an' follow me!
   Oh, 'ark to the big drum callin',
   Follow me -- follow me 'ome!

'Is mare she neighs the 'ole day long,
  She paws the 'ole night through,
An' she won't take 'er feed 'cause o' waitin' for 'is step,
  Which is just what a beast would do.

'Is girl she goes with a bombardier
  Before 'er month is through;
An' the banns are up in church, for she's got the beggar hooked,
  Which is just what a girl would do.

We fought 'bout a dog -- last week it were --
  No more than a round or two;
But I strook 'im cruel 'ard, an' I wish I 'adn't now,
  Which is just what a man can't do.

'E was all that I 'ad in the way of a friend,
  An' I've 'ad to find one new;
But I'd give my pay an' stripe for to get the beggar back,
  Which it's just too late to do.

  So it's knock out your pipes an' follow me!
  An' it's finish off your swipes an' follow me!
   Oh, 'ark to the fifes a-crawlin'!
   Follow me -- follow me 'ome!

   Take 'im away! 'E's gone where the best men go.
   Take 'im away! An' the gun-wheels turnin' slow.
   Take 'im away! There's more from the place 'e come.
   Take 'im away, with the limber an' the drum.

  For it's "Three rounds blank" an' follow me,
  An' it's "Thirteen rank" an' follow me;
   Oh, passin' the love o' women,
   Follow me -- follow me 'ome!

The Sergeant's Weddin'

'E was warned agin' 'er --
 That's what made 'im look;
She was warned agin' 'im --
 That is why she took.
'Wouldn't 'ear no reason,
 'Went an' done it blind;
We know all about 'em,
 They've got all to find!

    Cheer for the Sergeant's weddin' --
    Give 'em one cheer more!
    Grey gun-'orses in the lando,
    An' a rogue is married to, etc.

What's the use o' tellin'
 'Arf the lot she's been?
'E's a bloomin' robber,
 An' 'e keeps canteen.
'Ow did 'e get 'is buggy?
 Gawd, you needn't ask!
'Made 'is forty gallon
 Out of every cask!

Watch 'im, with 'is 'air cut,
 Count us filin' by --
Won't the Colonel praise 'is
 Pop -- u -- lar -- i -- ty!
We 'ave scores to settle --
 Scores for more than beer;
She's the girl to pay 'em --
 That is why we're 'ere!

See the chaplain thinkin'?
 See the women smile?
Twig the married winkin'
 As they take the aisle?
Keep your side-arms quiet,
 Dressin' by the Band.
Ho! You 'oly beggars,
 Cough be'ind your 'and!

Now it's done an' over,
 'Ear the organ squeak,
"'Voice that breathed o'er Eden" --
 Ain't she got the cheek!
White an' laylock ribbons,
 Think yourself so fine!
I'd pray Gawd to take yer
 'Fore I made yer mine!

Escort to the kerridge,
 Wish 'im luck, the brute!
Chuck the slippers after --
 (Pity 'tain't a boot!)
Bowin' like a lady,
 Blushin' like a lad --
'Oo would say to see 'em
 Both is rotten bad?

> Cheer for the Sergeant's weddin' --
> Give 'em one cheer more!
> Grey gun-'orses in the lando,
> An' a rogue is married to, etc.

The Jacket

Through the Plagues of Egyp' we was chasin' Arabi,
  Gettin' down an' shovin' in the sun;
An' you might 'ave called us dirty, an' you might ha' called us dry,
  An' you might 'ave 'eard us talkin' at the gun.
But the Captain 'ad 'is jacket, an' the jacket it was new --
  ('Orse Gunners, listen to my song!)
An' the wettin' of the jacket is the proper thing to do,
  Nor we didn't keep 'im waitin' very long.

One day they gave us orders for to shell a sand redoubt,
  Loadin' down the axle-arms with case;
But the Captain knew 'is dooty, an' he took the crackers out
  An' he put some proper liquor in its place.
An' the Captain saw the shrapnel, which is six-an'-thirty clear.
  ('Orse Gunners, listen to my song!)
"Will you draw the weight," sez 'e, "or will you draw the beer?"
  An' we didn't keep 'im waitin' very long.
    For the Captain, etc.

Then we trotted gentle, not to break the bloomin' glass,
  Though the Arabites 'ad all their ranges marked;
But we dursn't 'ardly gallop, for the most was bottled Bass,
  An' we'd dreamed of it since we was disembarked:
So we fired economic with the shells we 'ad in 'and,
  ('Orse Gunners, listen to my song!)
But the beggars under cover 'ad the impidence to stand,
  An' we couldn't keep 'em waitin' very long.
    And the Captain, etc.

So we finished 'arf the liquor (an' the Captain took champagne),
  An' the Arabites was shootin' all the while;
An' we left our wounded 'appy with the empties on the plain,
  An' we used the bloomin' guns for pro-jec-tile!
We limbered up an' galloped -- there were nothin' else to do --
  ('Orse Gunners, listen to my song!)
An' the Battery came a-boundin' like a boundin' kangaroo,
  But they didn't watch us comin' very long.
    As the Captain, etc.

We was goin' most extended -- we was drivin' very fine,
  An' the Arabites were loosin' 'igh an' wide,
Till the Captain took the glassy with a rattlin' right incline,
  An' we dropped upon their 'eads the other side.
Then we give 'em quarter -- such as 'adn't up and cut,
  ('Orse Gunners, listen to my song!)
An' the Captain stood a limberful of fizzy -- somethin' Brutt,
  But we didn't leave it fizzing very long.
    For the Captain, etc.

We might ha' been court-martialled, but it all come out all right
　When they signalled us to join the main command.
There was every round expended, there was every gunner tight,
　An' the Captain waved a corkscrew in 'is 'and.
　　But the Captain 'ad 'is jacket, etc.

The 'Eathen

The 'eathen in 'is blindness bows down to wood an' stone;
'E don't obey no orders unless they is 'is own;
'E keeps 'is side-arms awful: 'e leaves 'em all about,
An' then comes up the regiment an' pokes the 'eathen out.

    All along o' dirtiness, all along o' mess,
    All along o' doin' things rather-more-or-less,
    All along of abby-nay, kul, an' hazar-ho,
    Mind you keep your rifle an' yourself jus' so!
The young recruit is 'aughty -- 'e draf's from Gawd knows where;
They bid 'im show 'is stockin's an' lay 'is mattress square;
'E calls it bloomin' nonsense -- 'e doesn't know no more --
An' then up comes 'is Company an' kicks 'im round the floor!

The young recruit is 'ammered -- 'e takes it very 'ard;
'E 'angs 'is 'ead an' mutters -- 'e sulks about the yard;
'E talks o' "cruel tyrants" 'e'll swing for by-an'-by,
An' the others 'ears an' mocks 'im, an' the boy goes orf to cry.

The young recruit is silly -- 'e thinks o' suicide;
'E's lost 'is gutter-devil; 'e 'asn't got 'is pride;
But day by day they kicks 'im, which 'elps 'im on a bit,
Till 'e finds 'isself one mornin' with a full an' proper kit.

    Gettin' clear o' dirtiness, gettin' done with mess,
    Gettin' shut o' doin' things rather-more-or-less;
    Not so fond of abby-nay, kul, nor hazar-ho,
    Learns to keep 'is rifle an' 'isself jus' so!

The young recruit is 'appy -- 'e throws a chest to suit;
You see 'im grow mustaches; you 'ear 'im slap 'is boot;
'E learns to drop the "bloodies" from every word 'e slings,
An' 'e shows an 'ealthy brisket when 'e strips for bars an' rings.

The cruel-tyrant-sergeants they watch 'im 'arf a year;
They watch 'im with 'is comrades, they watch 'im with 'is beer;
They watch 'im with the women at the regimental dance,
And the cruel-tyrant-sergeants send 'is name along for "Lance".

An' now 'e's 'arf o' nothin', an' all a private yet,
'Is room they up an' rags 'im to see what they will get;
They rags 'im low an' cunnin', each dirty trick they can,
But 'e learns to sweat 'is temper an' 'e learns to sweat 'is man.

An', last, a Colour-Sergeant, as such to be obeyed,
'E schools 'is men at cricket, 'e tells 'em on parade;
They sees 'em quick an' 'andy, uncommon set an' smart,
An' so 'e talks to orficers which 'ave the Core at 'eart.

'E learns to do 'is watchin' without it showin' plain;
'E learns to save a dummy, an' shove 'im straight again;
'E learns to check a ranker that's buyin' leave to shirk;
An' 'e learns to make men like 'im so they'll learn to like their work.

An' when it comes to marchin' he'll see their socks are right,
An' when it comes to action 'e shows 'em 'ow to sight;
'E knows their ways of thinkin' and just what's in their mind;
'E knows when they are takin' on an' when they've fell be'ind.

'E knows each talkin' corpril that leads a squad astray;
'E feels 'is innards 'eavin', 'is bowels givin' way;
'E sees the blue-white faces all tryin' 'ard to grin,
An' 'e stands an' waits an' suffers till it's time to cap 'em in.

An' now the hugly bullets come peckin' through the dust,
An' no one wants to face 'em, but every beggar must;
So, like a man in irons which isn't glad to go,
They moves 'em off by companies uncommon stiff an' slow.

Of all 'is five years' schoolin' they don't remember much
Excep' the not retreatin', the step an' keepin' touch.
It looks like teachin' wasted when they duck an' spread an' 'op,
But if 'e 'adn't learned 'em they'd be all about the shop!

An' now it's "'Oo goes backward?" an' now it's "'Oo comes on?"
And now it's "Get the doolies," an' now the captain's gone;
An' now it's bloody murder, but all the while they 'ear
'Is voice, the same as barrick drill, a-shepherdin' the rear.

'E's just as sick as they are, 'is 'eart is like to split,
But 'e works 'em, works 'em, works 'em till he feels 'em take the bit;
The rest is 'oldin' steady till the watchful bugles play,
An' 'e lifts 'em, lifts 'em, lifts 'em through the charge that wins the day!

    The 'eathen in 'is blindness bows down to wood an' stone;
    'E don't obey no orders unless they is 'is own;
    The 'eathen in 'is blindness must end where 'e began,
    But the backbone of the Army is the non-commissioned man!

    Keep away from dirtiness -- keep away from mess.
    Don't get into doin' things rather-more-or-less!
    Let's ha' done with abby-nay, kul, an' hazar-ho;
    Mind you keep your rifle an' yourself jus' so!

The Shut-Eye Sentry

Sez the Junior Orderly Sergeant
 To the Senior Orderly Man:
"Our Orderly Orf'cer's hokee-mut,
 You 'elp 'im all you can.
For the wine was old and the night is cold,
 An' the best we may go wrong,
So, 'fore 'e gits to the sentry-box,
 You pass the word along."

    So it was "Rounds! What Rounds?" at two of a frosty night,
     'E's 'oldin' on by the sergeant's sash, but, sentry, shut your eye.
    An' it was "Pass! All's well!" Oh, ain't 'e drippin' tight!
     'E'll need an affidavit pretty badly by-an'-by.

The moon was white on the barricks,
 The road was white an' wide,
An' the Orderly Orf'cer took it all,
 An' the ten-foot ditch beside.
An' the corporal pulled an' the sergeant pushed,
 An' the three they danced along,
But I'd shut my eyes in the sentry-box,
 So I didn't see nothin' wrong.

    Though it was "Rounds! What Rounds?" O corporal, 'old 'im up!
     'E's usin' 'is cap as it shouldn't be used, but, sentry, shut your eye.
    An' it was "Pass! All's well!" Ho, shun the foamin' cup!
     'E'll need, etc.

'Twas after four in the mornin';
 We 'ad to stop the fun,
An' we sent 'im 'ome on a bullock-cart,
 With 'is belt an' stock undone;
But we sluiced 'im down an' we washed 'im out,
 An' a first-class job we made,
When we saved 'im, smart as a bombardier,
 For six-o'clock parade.

    It 'ad been "Rounds! What Rounds?" Oh, shove 'im straight again!
     'E's usin' 'is sword for a bicycle, but, sentry, shut your eye.
    An' it was "Pass! All's well!" 'E's called me "Darlin' Jane"!
     'E'll need, etc.

The drill was long an' 'eavy,
 The sky was 'ot an' blue,
An' 'is eye was wild an' 'is 'air was wet,
 But 'is sergeant pulled 'im through.
Our men was good old trusties --
 They'd done it on their 'ead;
But you ought to 'ave 'eard 'em markin' time

To 'ide the things 'e said!

> For it was "Right flank -- wheel!" for "'Alt, an' stand at ease!"
> An' "Left extend!" for "Centre close!" O marker, shut your eye!
> An' it was, "'Ere, sir, 'ere! before the Colonel sees!"
> So he needed affidavits pretty badly by-an'-by.

There was two-an'-thirty sergeants,
  There was corp'rals forty-one,
There was just nine 'undred rank an' file
  To swear to a touch o' sun.
There was me 'e'd kissed in the sentry-box,
  As I 'ave not told in my song,
But I took my oath, which were Bible truth,
  I 'adn't seen nothin' wrong.

There's them that's 'ot an' 'aughty,
  There's them that's cold an' 'ard,
But there comes a night when the best gets tight,
  And then turns out the Guard.
I've seen them 'ide their liquor
  In every kind o' way,
But most depends on makin' friends
  With Privit Thomas A.!

> When it is "Rounds! What Rounds?" 'E's breathin' through 'is nose.
> 'E's reelin', rollin', roarin' tight, but, sentry, shut your eye.
> An' it is "Pass! All's well!" An' that's the way it goes:
> We'll 'elp 'im for 'is mother, an' 'e'll 'elp us by-an'-by!

'Mary, Pity Women!'

You call yourself a man,
 For all you used to swear,
An' leave me, as you can,
 My certain shame to bear?
 I 'ear! You do not care --
You done the worst you know.
 I 'ate you, grinnin' there. . . .
Ah, Gawd, I love you so!

> Nice while it lasted, an' now it is over --
> Tear out your 'eart an' good-bye to your lover!
> What's the use o' grievin', when the mother that bore you
> (Mary, pity women!) knew it all before you?

It aren't no false alarm,
 The finish to your fun;
You -- you 'ave brung the 'arm,
 An' I'm the ruined one;
 An' now you'll off an' run
With some new fool in tow.
 Your 'eart? You 'aven't none. . . .
Ah, Gawd, I love you so!

> When a man is tired there is naught will bind 'im;
> All 'e solemn promised 'e will shove be'ind 'im.
> What's the good o' prayin' for The Wrath to strike 'im
> (Mary, pity women!), when the rest are like 'im?

What 'ope for me or -- it?
 What's left for us to do?
I've walked with men a bit,
 But this -- but this is you.
So 'elp me Christ, it's true!
 Where can I 'ide or go?
You coward through and through! . . .
 Ah, Gawd, I love you so!

> All the more you give 'em the less are they for givin' --
> Love lies dead, an' you cannot kiss 'im livin'.
> Down the road 'e led you there is no returnin'
> (Mary, pity women!), but you're late in learnin'!

You'd like to treat me fair?
 You can't, because we're pore?
We'd starve? What do I care!
 We might, but this is shore!
 I want the name -- no more --
The name, an' lines to show,
 An' not to be an 'ore. . . .

Ah, Gawd, I love you so!

What's the good o' pleadin', when the mother that bore you
(Mary, pity women!) knew it all before you?
Sleep on 'is promises an' wake to your sorrow
(Mary, pity women!), for we sail to-morrow!

For to Admire

The Injian Ocean sets an' smiles
 So sof', so bright, so bloomin' blue;
There aren't a wave for miles an' miles
 Excep' the jiggle from the screw.
The ship is swep', the day is done,
 The bugle's gone for smoke and play;
An' black agin' the settin' sun
 The Lascar sings, "Hum deckty hai!"

   For to admire an' for to see,
    For to be'old this world so wide --
   It never done no good to me,
    But I can't drop it if I tried!

I see the sergeants pitchin' quoits,
 I 'ear the women laugh an' talk,
I spy upon the quarter-deck
 The orficers an' lydies walk.
I thinks about the things that was,
 An' leans an' looks acrost the sea,
Till spite of all the crowded ship
 There's no one lef' alive but me.

The things that was which I 'ave seen,
 In barrick, camp, an' action too,
I tells them over by myself,
 An' sometimes wonders if they're true;
For they was odd -- most awful odd --
 But all the same now they are o'er,
There must be 'eaps o' plenty such,
 An' if I wait I'll see some more.

Oh, I 'ave come upon the books,
 An' frequent broke a barrick rule,
An' stood beside an' watched myself
 Be'avin' like a bloomin' fool.
I paid my price for findin' out,
 Nor never grutched the price I paid,
But sat in Clink without my boots,
 Admirin' 'ow the world was made.

Be'old a crowd upon the beam,
 An' 'umped above the sea appears
Old Aden, like a barrick-stove
 That no one's lit for years an' years!
I passed by that when I began,
 An' I go 'ome the road I came,
A time-expired soldier-man
 With six years' service to 'is name.

My girl she said, "Oh, stay with me!"
 My mother 'eld me to 'er breast.
They've never written none, an' so
 They must 'ave gone with all the rest --
With all the rest which I 'ave seen
 An' found an' known an' met along.
I cannot say the things I feel,
 And so I sing my evenin' song:

> For to admire an' for to see,
> For to be'old this world so wide --
> It never done no good to me,
> But I can't drop it if I tried!